Sky-High Guy

Nina Crews

Christy Ottaviano Books
Henry Holt and Company
New York

Henry Holt and Company, LLC, *Publishers since 1866*
175 Fifth Avenue, New York, New York 10010 [www.HenryHoltKids.com]

Henry Holt® is a registered trademark of Henry Holt and Company, LLC.
Distributed in Canada by H. B. Fenn and Company Ltd.

Library of Congress Cataloging-in-Publication Data
Crews, Nina.
Sky-high Guy / by Nina Crews. — 1st ed.
p.   cm.
"Christy Ottaviano Books."
Summary: Jack likes to play with his "friend" Guy without the interference of his little brother Gus, but when Guy gets stuck in a tree,
Gus is the perfect companion to help Jack rescue him.
ISBN 978-0-8050-8764-2
[1. Toys—Fiction. 2. Brothers—Fiction. 3. Play—Fiction.] I. Title. PZ7.C8683Sk 2010   [E]—dc22   2009012218

First Edition—2010
The artist used digitally color-corrected and -manipulated 35 mm color photographs, line drawings,
and black-and-white photographs to create the illustrations for this book.
Printed in October 2009 in China by Macmillan Production (Asia) Ltd., Kwun Tong, Kowloon, Hong Kong (Supplier Code: 10). ∞

10 9 8 7 6 5 4 3 2 1

To Hazel

Thank you, Jack Rader and Gus Rader,
for starring in this book. You did a great job!
Also thanks to Amy Crews for your assistance and enthusiasm.

Jack and Guy had many adventures.
Sometimes Jack's little brother, Gus, joined them.

But Jack mostly liked to play with Guy by himself. They were a team.

Jack and Guy trekked to a magical island to hunt dinosaurs.

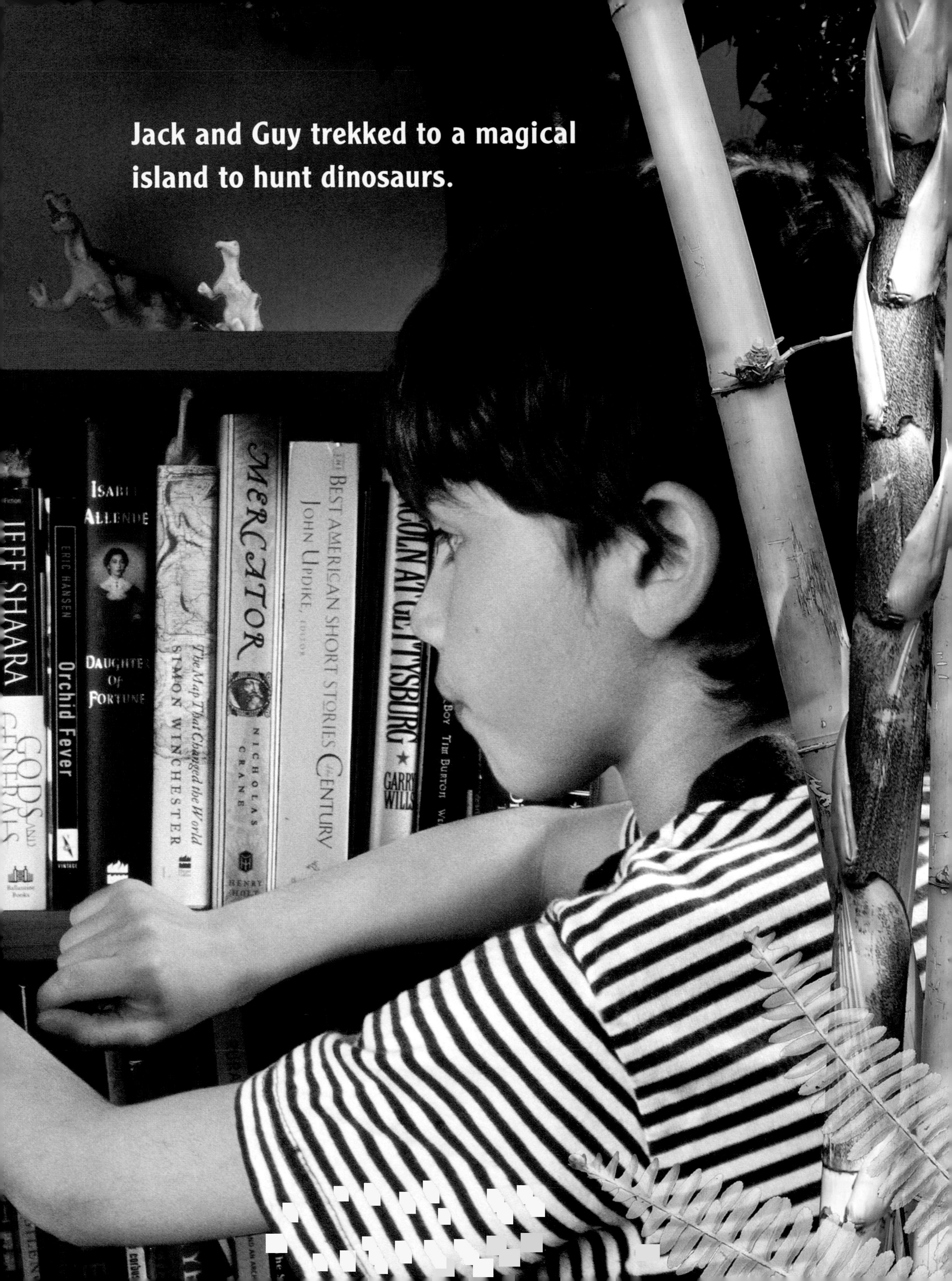

Jack and Guy were superheroes— saving the city from destruction.

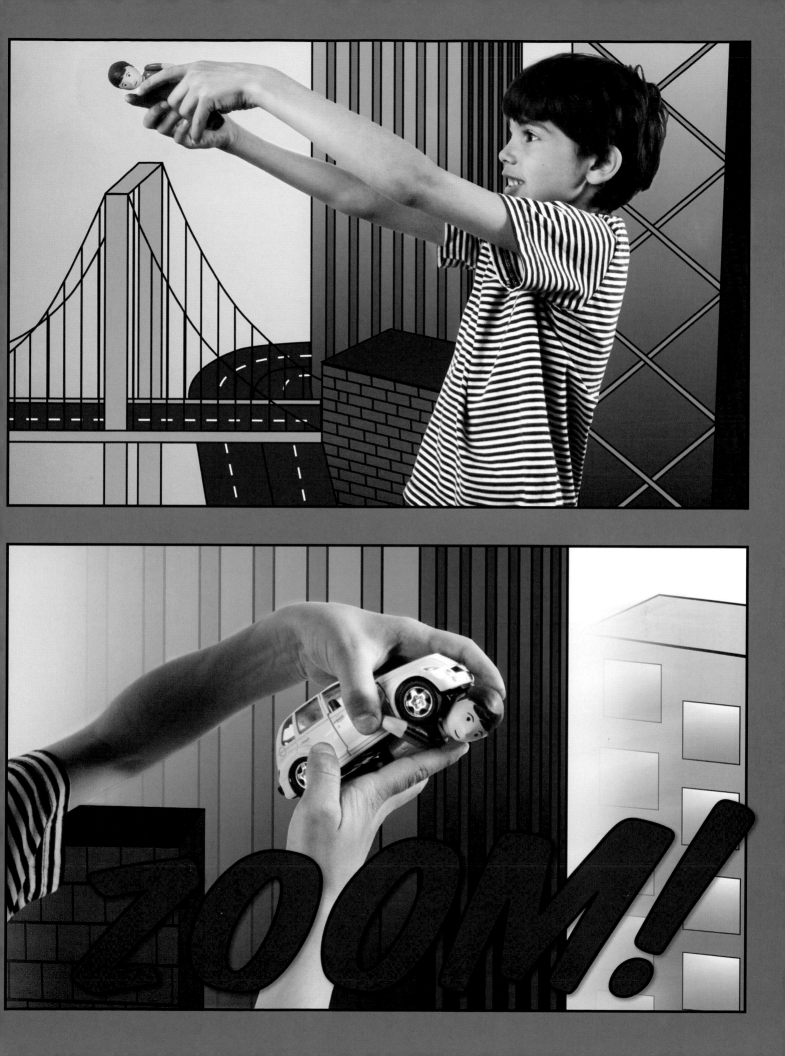

Jack and Guy went
skydiving!

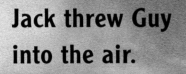

Up!

Jack threw Guy
into the air.

Down he came, landing
safely in the field.

Up
again!

Up!

Down he landed on
the rocky beachfront.

Down Guy
landed in
city traffic!
Oops!

Up. Down. Up. Down.
Guy flew higher and higher—
brushing the treetops.

Until Guy got caught
in a high tree branch.

"Oh, no!"
cried Jack and Gus.

Jack tried to reach Guy.
Gus wanted to help.
Guy was really stuck.

"Boys, come inside,"
called their mother.

Guy wouldn't want to be left alone.

It could rain or snow.

Wild animals could bother him.

The next day Jack gathered everything
that he might need to rescue Guy.
He found a rope, a pail, and his
binoculars. Then he asked Gus
to help him.

"C'mon, Gus. We've got
to rescue Guy!"

Gus looked through the binoculars.
Guy needed help now.
Jack made a lasso.
He threw it over and over again.

Finally he caught the right branch.
Jack and Gus lowered it.

"Gus! We've almost got him!"
Jack shouted.

Gus held the rope tight, while Jack
freed Guy from the tree leaves.

"Yeah!"
they shouted.

"Gus!" said Jack.
"We saved Guy!"

That afternoon Jack, Gus,
and Guy explored the
rain forest together.
They made a great team.
"Look out for snakes!"
said Jack.